AR 2.9   .5PT   5/99

HALLOWEEN

by Joyce K. Kessel
pictures by Nancy L. Carlson

Carolrhoda Books
Minneapolis, Minnesota

LIBRARY OF CONGRESS CATALOGING IN PUBLICATION DATA

Kessel, Joyce K.
Halloween.

(On my own books)
SUMMARY: Explains the origins of the holiday of Halloween and such traditions as black cats, jack-o-lanterns, witches,
bonfires, and trick-or-treating.

1. Halloween—Juvenile literature. [1. Halloween] I. Carlson,
Nancy L. II. Title.

GT4965.K47   394.2′683   80-15890
ISBN 0-87614-132-7   (lib. bdg.)

3   4   5   6   7   8   9   10   85   84   83

to Dad and Dee
—J. K. K.

to my mother and father
—N. L. C.

Fall has always been

a special time of year.

It is a time to give thanks.

The crops are in.

There is enough food for all.

But hundreds of years ago
fall was also a time to feel afraid.
People felt the sun grow weaker.
They watched the days grow shorter.
They saw plants dying.

Long ago that frightened people.
They thought evil powers
were pushing the sun away.

The Celts were people

who lived over 2,000 years ago.

Most of them lived

in Great Britain and Ireland.

The Celts had many gods.

One was named Samhain.

He was the god of death.

His special night was October 31.

That was the Celts' New Year's Eve.

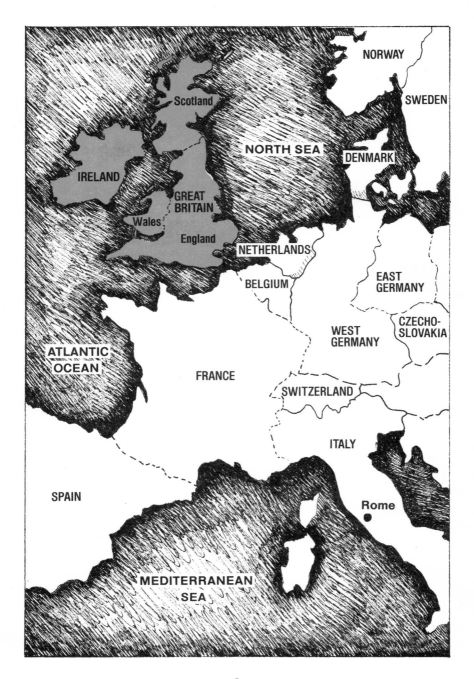

NORWAY

SWEDEN

Scotland

NORTH SEA

DENMARK

IRELAND

GREAT
BRITAIN

Wales

England

NETHERLANDS

BELGIUM

EAST
GERMANY

CZECHO-
SLOVAKIA

WEST
GERMANY

ATLANTIC
OCEAN

FRANCE

SWITZERLAND

ITALY

SPAIN

Rome

MEDITERRANEAN
SEA

The Celts believed

Samhain came to earth that night.

He let the dead come back too.

The Celts made large fires.

They burned animals as gifts for Samhain.

Some of them wore costumes
made from animals' heads and furs.
Samhain's night was a frightening time.
It marked the beginning of winter.
It became the beginning of our Halloween.

In the year 43,

the Romans conquered the Celts.

The Romans also had many gods.

One was named Pomona.

She was the goddess of fruit.

Her festival was in the fall.

It came right after Samhain's night.

But Pomona's festival was a happy time.

It was a time to give thanks

to all the gods.

Apples were important to Pomona.

So Romans gave apples

to their gods of rain and fire.

They wanted to thank them

for not harming the crops.

The Romans ruled the Celts
for about 400 years.
During that time
Pomona's and Samhain's festivals
got mixed up.
They became one festival.
And today apples are still
an important part of Halloween.

In the 1800s,

many people moved to the United States.

Some came from

Great Britain and Ireland.

That was where the Celts had lived.

They brought their holidays with them.

One of those holidays was Halloween.

BLACK CATS

Think of all the black cats
you see on Halloween.
Black cats
standing beside jack-o-lanterns.
Black cats on witches' brooms.
Some people think
black cats bring bad luck.

The Celts believed black cats
had once been people.
They thought bad magic
had changed them into cats.
They tied black cats with silver ropes.
They wanted to keep them.
The cats were supposed
to protect church treasures.

JACK-O-LANTERNS

We got our jack-o-lantern from Ireland.

The Irish tell a story

about a man named Jack.

Jack was very bad.

He could not go to heaven.

So he was sent to hell.

But he played too many tricks there.

The devil got angry.

Finally the devil sent Jack

out of hell too.

Poor Jack.

He had no place to go.

He had to walk the earth forever.

All he owned was a little lantern.

The Irish called him

"Jack of the Lantern."

Now when we cut lanterns in pumpkins,

we call them jack-o-lanterns.

TRICK-OR-TREATING

Trick-or-treating

came from Ireland too.

Long ago people believed in ghosts.

Clever Irish farmers made use of that.

They went to rich homes.

They asked for food.

If the rich people would not give any,

the farmers played tricks on them.

They might steal a gate.

They might move a wagon far away.

People thought ghosts

had played the tricks.

"We should be nicer," they said.

"Then the ghosts will leave us alone."

So they gave food to the farmers.

And the ghosts stayed away!

GHOSTS

A ghost is a spirit of a dead person
that visits a living person.
Most people today
do not believe in ghosts.
But long ago most people did.
Ghosts have been part of Halloween
from its very beginning.

The Celts believed
ghosts visited earth on October 31.
People in other countries
also came to believe this.

There is a big cave in Ireland.

It is called the "Hell-Gate of Ireland."

People once believed

this cave opened on Halloween.

Horrible ghosts flew out of it.

People thought the ghosts killed animals.

They believed the ghosts took babies too.

WITCHES

A witch is a woman with magic powers.
Once the word *witch* could mean
a man or a woman.
Today witches who are men
are called warlocks.

In Scotland people once believed
all witches met on Halloween.
The devil called them together.
They danced all night.

Music was played
on the "devil's bagpipe."
This bagpipe was made
from hens' heads and cats' tails!

APPLES

We have seen how apples
became part of Halloween
when the Romans conquered the Celts.
Today there are many apple games
we can play on Halloween.

In Ireland

Halloween is called "Apple Night."

People tie strings to apples.

They hang them from the ceiling.

Everyone takes turns.

They stand on a chair.

The apples swing back and forth.

The trick is to take a bite of one.

But you can't use your hands.

In Wales people bob for apples.

Apples are put in a tub of water.

People try to catch one

in their teeth.

They hold their hands

behind their backs.

A favorite game in the United States

is passing an apple

from one person to another.

You can't use your hands

in this game either.

You must hold the apple under your chin!

FORTUNE-TELLING

Have you ever had your fortune told?

Maybe someone has "read your palm."

Other people "read" tea leaves.

Fortune-tellers tell people

what might happen to them.

The Celts told fortunes
by looking through what was left
of burned animals.
These animals had been burned
as gifts for Samhain.

The Celts believed
the fortunes they told.
Today we tell fortunes at Halloween too.
But we don't really believe them.
We do it for fun.
The English call Halloween
"Nutcrack Night."
Sweethearts throw nuts into the fire.
Sometimes they explode.
That means a bad marriage.
Sometimes they burn quietly.
That means a good marriage.

39

The Irish hide rings in food.

If you find the ring,

you will marry soon.

BONFIRES

Have you ever been

to a Halloween bonfire?

The fire crackles.

It feels warm.

It smells good.

People sing songs.

They tell ghost stories.

It is a happy time.

But bonfires used to be very serious.

The Celts burned them for Samhain.

Later people burned bonfires

all over Great Britain and Ireland

on Halloween.

They did this to frighten

ghosts and witches away.

In Scotland people burned torches.

Then they ran through the streets.

They were trying to frighten witches.

Later they made a big fire

with all the torches.

Then a man dressed up like a ghost.

He rode up on a horse.

The horse pulled a wagon.

In the wagon was a make-believe witch.

The people screamed.

They threw the witch into the fire!

While the witch burned, they danced.

People in Wales burned bonfires too.

Each person would mark a stone.

They threw the stones into the fire.

Sometimes a stone was missing

the next morning.

People thought

the person who marked the missing stone

would die that year.

Today the early reasons for Halloween
have disappeared.
Few people still believe
the dead come back.
But we carry on some of the old customs.

It's fun to pretend

we believe in witches and ghosts.

It's fun to tell scary stories

and go trick-or-treating.

It's fun to tell fortunes

even if we don't really believe them.

In October the dry leaves
whisper like witches.
Our bright jack-o-lanterns
smile at our windows.
Today Halloween is a happy way
to say hello to winter.